The Teeny Weeny Tadpole

For Veronica and Rye Mepham
at the Rescuers Wildlife Sanctuary —S.C.

For Ethan —J.T.

ISBN 0-439-85449-0

Based on the title "Look Out for the Big Bad Fish!" written by Sheridan
Cain and illustrated by Tanya Linch by Little Tiger Press. Text copyright
© 2005 by Little Tiger Press. Illustrations copyright © 2005 by Jack Tickle.
All rights reserved. Published by Scholastic Inc., 557 Broadway, New York,
NY 10012, by arrangement with Tiger Tales, an imprint of ME Media, LLC.
SCHOLASTIC and associated logos are trademarks and/or registered
trademarks of Scholastic Inc.

12 11 10 9 8 7 6 5 4 3 2 1   6 7 8 9 10 11/0

Printed in the U.S.A.   08

First Scholastic printing, March 2006

The Teeny Weeny Tadpole

by Sheridan Cain

Illustrated by Jack Tickle

SCHOLASTIC INC.
New York Toronto London Auckland Sydney
Mexico City New Delhi Hong Kong Buenos Aires

The Teeny Weeny Tadpole swam in and out of the lily pads. Splish! Splash! "Hello, my busy little tadpole," said Mommy Frog. "It's such a nice day for splashing and leaping…"

Boing!

Mommy Frog jumped
high into the air.

Flippity-flop!

She landed with a plop!
"I can do that!" said the Teeny
Weeny Tadpole, and he tried to leap
onto a lily pad. All he managed was
a splish and a splash.

"Mom, why can't I jump like you?" asked the Teeny Weeny Tadpole.

"Oh, you will, Tadpole," said Mommy Frog. "Just keep splishing and splashing."

The Teeny Weeny Tadpole swam off downstream. "Be careful, Tadpole," called Mommy Frog. "Look out for the Big Bad Fish!"

The Teeny Weeny Tadpole wiggled his way to the edge of the stream to splash among the water lilies. He looked up and saw a woolly face with a smudgy nose.

"Hello," said Tadpole. "Who are you?"

"I'm Lamb," said the woolly-faced animal.

"Can you jump?" asked Tadpole.

"You bet!" said Lamb. "Watch this!"

Boing!

Lamb jumped
high into the air.

Springity-sproing!

He landed with a boing!
"Oh!" said the Teeny Weeny Tadpole.
"I wish I could jump like that."
"Oh, you will, Tadpole," said Lamb.
"Soon you will."

A few days later, the Teeny Weeny Tadpole paddled downstream to where the violets tickled his tummy. He looked up and saw a twitchy nose and the largest pair of ears he'd ever seen.

"Hello," said Tadpole. "Who are you?"

"I'm Rabbit," said the twitchy-nosed animal.

"Can you jump?" asked Tadpole.

"Can I jump?" said Rabbit.
"Watch this!"

Rabbit jumped high into the air.

Jumpity-jump.!

Rabbit landed with a thump!
"Wow," said the Teeny Weeny
Tadpole. "I wish I could jump
like that."

"Oh, you will, Tadpole," said
Rabbit. "Very soon, you will."

Several days later, the Teeny Weeny Tadpole swam
out to where the tall grass waved in the wind. He saw
a pair of bug eyes and two springy legs.
"Hello," said Tadpole. "Who are you?"
"I'm Grasshopper," said the buggy-eyed creature.
"Can you jump?" asked Tadpole.

"Of course," said Grasshopper.
"Watch this!"

Boing!

Grasshopper jumped high into the air.

Hippity-hop!

Grasshopper landed with a bop!
"Whoa," said the Teeny Weeny
Tadpole. "I wish I could jump like that."
"Oh, you will, Tadpole," said
Grasshopper. "Very soon, you will."

The next time the Teeny Weeny Tadpole went exploring, he swam far out to where the stream widened and the water became still. Tadpole looked down and saw a pair of huge, rubbery lips.

"Hello," said Tadpole. "Who are you?"
"Hello," boomed the rubbery-lipped creature.
"I'm the Big Bad Fish, and

I EAT TADPOLES!"

The Big Bad Fish
chased the Teeny
Weeny Tadpole up...

and down...

and in and out
of the weeds...

getting
closer
and
closer
until...

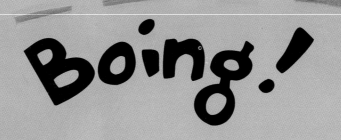

Boing!

The Teeny Weeny Tadpole leaped high into the air, higher than Lamb, higher than Rabbit, and higher than Grasshopper. He leaped all the way home.

"Look, Mommy!" said Tadpole.
"I can jump just like you!"
His mother smiled proudly.
"Of course you can, my little FROG!"

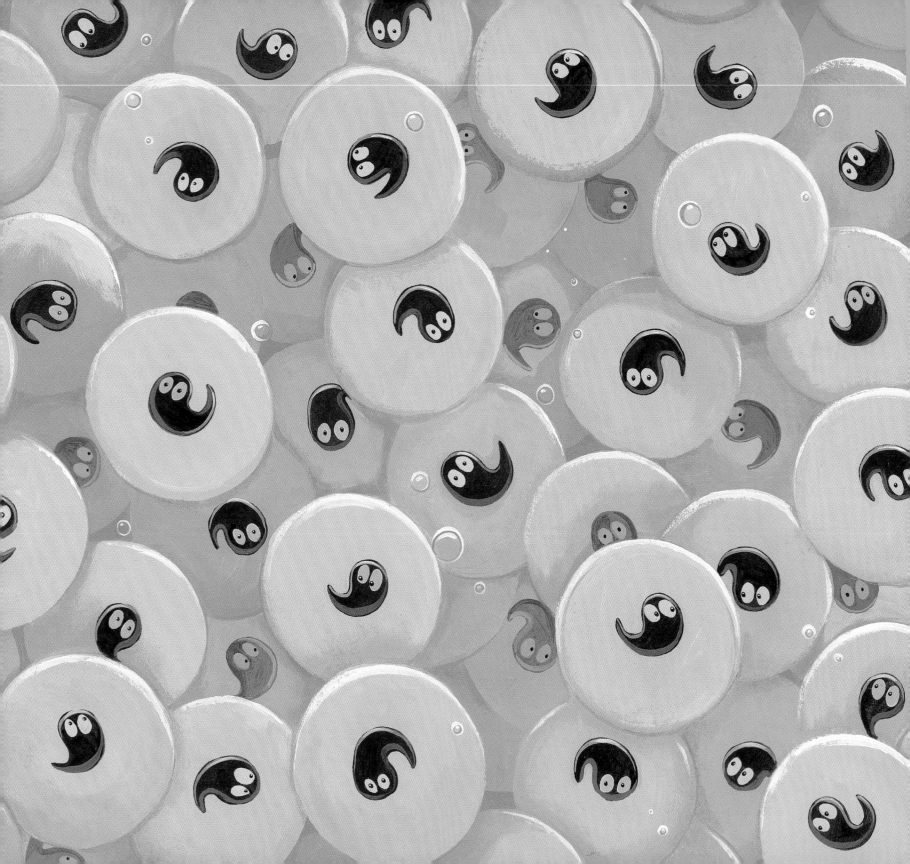